SAND CASTLE

BY Brenda Shannon Yee
PICTURES BY Thea Kliros

Greenwillow Books, New York

Watercolors and pencil were used for the full-color art.
The text type is Della Robbia.
Text copyright © 1999 by Brenda Shannon Yee
Illustrations copyright © 1999 by Thea Kliros
Printed in Singapore by Tien Wah Press
First Edition
10 9 8 7 6 5 4 3 2 1

Library of Congress Cataloging-in-Publication Data

Yee, Brenda Shannon.
Sand castle / Brenda Shannon Yee ; pictures by Thea Kliros.
    p.   cm.
Summary: Jen starts to build a sand castle at the beach, and others
come along to help make the moat, path, wall, and road around it.
ISBN 0-688-16194-4
[1. Sandcastles–Fiction.   2. Beaches–Fiction.]   I. Kliros, Thea, ill.
II. Title.   PZ7.Y363San   1999   [E]–dc21   98-24272   CIP   AC

FOR MY BEST SAND CASTLE BUDDIES—
CAITY, CAROLYN, AND BOB
— B. S. Y.

FOR FELIX, LOTTE, AND KYLA
— T. K.

Jen dug the sand with her shovel.
A boy with a bucket watched.
"Can I help?" he asked.
"I am building a sand castle," said Jen.

"Your castle needs a moat," said the boy.
He dug a circle around Jen's castle
with his bucket.

The castle grew taller.
The moat grew deeper.

"Can I help?" asked a girl with a spoon.
"I am making the moat," said the boy.
"This is my castle," said Jen.

"If I dig a path to the lake, the moat will fill up with water," the girl said.

She scooped a path in the sand.
Water sloshed into the path and
headed toward the moat.

The castle grew taller.
The moat grew deeper.
The path grew wider.

"Can I help?" asked a boy with a cup.
"I am digging the path to the water," said the girl.

"I am making the moat," said the boy.
"This is my castle," said Jen.

"You will need a wall to protect your
castle," said the boy with the cup.
The boy filled the cup with wet sand.
Pat, pat. He turned it over.
Tap, tap. One sand block stood.
Pat, tap. Two sand blocks.

The castle grew taller.
The moat grew deeper.
The path grew wider.
The wall grew longer.

"Can I help?" asked a girl holding a rake.

"I am building the wall," said the boy
with the cup.
"I am digging the path to the water,"
said the girl with the spoon.
"I am making the moat," said the boy
with the bucket.
"This is my castle," said Jen.

"You need a road, so people can get to the castle," said the girl with the rake. Dragging the rake in the sand, the girl traced a winding road. With the rake teeth, she swirled wavy shapes.

Hands patted and pushed the squishy sand.
The castle rose high.
The moat dipped deep.
The path flowed long.
The wall stood strong.
The road lay wide and welcoming.

Shadows stretched across the sand.
"Angela! Time to go!"
"Robert! We're leaving!"
"Tanisha! It's late!"
"Louis! Rinse your feet!"
"Jen! Say good-bye!"

"But what about the castle?
We worked so hard," Tanisha said.
"As soon as we leave, someone
will wreck it," said Louis.

"I know what to do!" Jen said.
Splat! She jumped on the castle.

In a flurry they all kicked the road,
toppled the wall, flattened the path,
filled the moat, and crushed the castle.

"Good-bye!" the beach friends shouted
as they scattered across the cooling sand.
"Let's do it again tomorrow!"